Marta Kočí

KATIE'S KITTEN

NEUGEBAUER PRESS U·S·A·

Far away in the mountains,
hidden under drifts of deep snow,
is Katie's house.
She lives here quite happily all by herself.
She is not lonely, though,
because she shares her home with
a kitten named Purr, a fat pink pig,
a little brown speckled hen, and a family of mice.

Every morning Katie sets the table,
and when the porridge is ready, she calls:
"Kitten, kitten, breakfast is on the table."
The hen always shares her bowl
with one of the mice on the floor,
while Katie and Purr eat together at the table.
Katie eats her porridge politely with a spoon.
She always gives Purr a spoon, too.
But he laps his food right up from the bowl,
because that is just what kittens
are supposed to do.

One morning after breakfast,
Katie could not get to the barn to do her chores.
The wind that she had heard blowing
the night before had brought fresh snow,
and the path to the barn was buried deep.
The pig was hungry and waiting for his breakfast,
so Katie worked hard to shovel the snow away.
Purr waited on the doorstep
until the path was clear.

Katie fed the pig and put clean straw
into a corner of the pigpen.
Then she chopped the firewood into small pieces.

When the chopping was done,
Katie put her hat and coat back on and said,
"Now I must go to school, Purr.
Don't you run away while I'm gone, little cat."

Whoosh!
Katie whizzed down the hill to her school
faster than ever before.
The kitten tried to follow the tracks of her skis,
but the snow got deeper and deeper,
and soon Purr was left behind all alone.

Purr's little paws were nearly frozen
and he could not find his way home.
When he saw a pile of chopped wood, he thought,
"That must be the barn!
And there's a light burning,
just as it does at home."
But it was only some woodcutters,
huddling over their fire as they ate their lunch.
And behind a fallen tree were two fierce dogs
who bared their teeth and growled at the kitten.

Purr ran away
and the big dogs chased him through the woods
and across the snow-covered fields.

With a frightened "Miaow!"
Purr leaped up into a tall tree.
As he sat there just out of reach,
he trembled and wished that Katie
would come and save him.

At last the dogs got bored and went away,
but Purr stayed in the tree.
He could not forget their sharp teeth
and long pink tongues, and how loudly
they had barked and snarled at him.
Suddenly a big dark shadow loomed over him.
An owl!
He jumped down from the tree
and ran away as fast as he could.

When Katie came home from school
she looked everywhere for her kitten.
"Purr, Purr," she called,
"where are you? Where are you hiding?"
She searched the whole house
from the cellar to the attic,
but there was no sign of him.
Katie started to cry.

By this time Katie's little kitten
had stumbled into a deep snowdrift
and fallen asleep.
He didn't know that Katie was looking for him,
and as he slept, he had a terrible nightmare.

He dreamed that a huge bear with tiger's teeth
had found him in the snow and was gobbling him up.

Just as Purr was dreaming
that the bear had swallowed him,
he heard a familiar voice calling.
And it was not a dream!
Katie ran towards him and cried out:
"There you are, my poor little Purr!"

Far away in the mountains,
in Katie's little house,
a light burned late into the night.
She and her kitten were having a midnight feast.

And when Purr had eaten
so much cream and hot apple pie
that he felt warm and comfortable again,
he began to feel sleepy, too.
Soon Katie and her kitten were fast asleep.